FERNANDA EMEDIATO

Illustrated by
VANESSA ALEXANDRE

THE PANDA BEAR AND THE ANT

Translation by
Luara Lopes

I hope you are filled with joy and curiosity because I have something very special to share with you. Let's talk about the marvelous Chinese bamboo and its incredible journey of growth! Did you know that after planting a Chinese bamboo seed, approximately five years can pass with nothing visible happening above the ground? It's true! During that time, something magical is unfolding, but totally hidden beneath the earth.

You see, as time goes by, a complex network of roots begins to form. These roots extend vertically and horizontally through the soil, like a secret labyrinth. They are working diligently to ensure that the bamboo grows strong and healthy. Then, at the end of the fifth year, something incredible happens: the Chinese bamboo begins to emerge from the ground, rapidly growing to an astonishing height of 25 meters! It's as if it has been storing all its strength and energy during those underground years, ready to amaze everyone with its grandeur.

It is in this magnificent bamboo grove that the fascinating story of the panda bear and the ant unfolds, an unusual encounter between an imposing character and a courageous one.

Shall we embark on this journey together?

With love, **The Author**

ONCE UPON A TIME, IN A LUSH BAMBOO GROVE, WHERE NATURE PAINTED A SPECTACLE OF COLORS AND LIFE. AMIDST THE TALL AND ELEGANT STALKS, A HUNGRY PANDA BEAR DISCOVERED THE MOST VIGOROUS AND DELICIOUS BAMBOO STEM HE HAD EVER SEEN.

The bear eagerly opened his mouth, about to savor that delicacy of the gods. However, to his surprise, he spotted a small, brave, and fearless ant that had made the bamboo its home.

THE BEAR ISSUED HIS FIRST WARNING, TELLING THE ANT TO GET OUT OF HIS WAY, FOR HIS APPETITE WAS FIERCE. BUT THE ANT, STEADFAST AND DETERMINED, RETORTED THAT SHE HAD ARRIVED FIRST AND HAD NO INTENTION OF BACKING DOWN.

THE BEAR, IRRITATED AND BARING HIS TEETH, BELLOWED DETERMINEDLY, TRYING TO MAKE THE ANT RECONSIDER HER POSITION.

BUT THE LITTLE ANT, UNSHAKEN, STUCK OUT HER TONGUE, DEFYING HIM WITH HER BOLD ATTITUDE.

DETERMINED TO MOVE FORWARD, THE BEAR OPENED HIS HUNGRY MAW ONCE AGAIN, READY TO DEVOUR THE BAMBOO STEM, ALONG WITH EVERY LEAF AND ANYTHING ELSE ON THEM.

That's when a colossal shout erupted through the air, causing all the birds to take flight in fright.

THE BEAR HAD RECEIVED A PAINFUL STING ON HIS TONGUE,

WHICH MADE HIM RUN IN DESPERATION
AND GIVE UP THE MEAL.

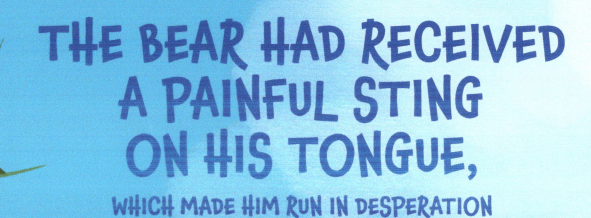

THE ANT, PROUD OF HER RESILIENCE AND CUNNING, EMERGED VICTORIOUS FROM THE CONFLICT. SHE SHOWED THE BEAR THAT TRUE STRENGTH LIES IN THE ABILITY TO RESIST AND GROW IN THE FACE OF CHALLENGES.

DID YOU KNOW?

Did you know that the giant panda lives in the mountains of China? Some of them are in the province of Sichuan. These beautiful mountains are full of bamboo, which is the panda's favorite food.

Both the panda and bamboo are very important elements of Chinese culture. The panda, considered a national treasure, is a beloved symbol of the country and represents the importance of protecting wildlife and nature. Bamboo, on the other hand, symbolizes virtues such as flexibility, resilience, humility, and integrity. It is also associated with longevity and wisdom.

Can you believe that pandas primarily eat bamboo? Yes, they are almost vegetarian! They consume an enormous amount of bamboo every day, about 40 kilograms! They are true bamboo-eating specialists. In Chinese forests, they feed on thirty different species of this plant.

Do you know what's curious about pandas? On their front paws, they have a kind of adapted "thumb." It's like having an extra finger! This helps them easily grasp the leaves and bamboo stalks.

Another incredible thing about pandas is that, thanks to their sharp claws, they are great at climbing trees. But most of the time, they prefer to stay on the ground, moving from one bamboo grove to another.

Each panda has a unique black and white spot pattern, just like a human fingerprint. This helps scientists identify and study pandas individually.

China makes a special effort to protect pandas. It has established a reserve and a national park just for these adorable animals. This way, they have a safe place to live and be happy.

These are some facts about pandas and bamboo in China. It's amazing how nature gives us such a special animal and a plant full of meaning. I hope you enjoyed learning about pandas and bamboo. Let's take care of nature and cherish the wonders it offers us!

ACTIVITIES Inspired by the STORY of
THE PANDA BEAR AND THE ANT:

1

DRAWING THE BEAR AND THE ANT: TAKE PAPER, COLORED PENCILS, OR CRAYONS AND DRAW THE BEAR AND THE ANT AS YOU IMAGINE THEY ARE LIKE. LET YOUR IMAGINATION RUN WILD AND BRING THE CHARACTERS FROM THE BOOK TO LIFE!

2

BAMBOO HUNT: LET'S PLAY A BAMBOO TREASURE HUNT! ASK AN ADULT TO HIDE SMALL PIECES OF BAMBOO AROUND THE HOUSE OR IN THE GARDEN. THEN, YOU'LL HAVE TO SEARCH AND COLLECT THEM ALL. WHOEVER FINDS THE MOST BAMBOO PIECES WINS!

3

SHADOW THEATER: YOU CAN CREATE A SHADOW THEATER AT HOME! GRAB A FLASHLIGHT AND CUT OUT SILHOUETTES OF A BEAR AND AN ANT FROM BLACK PAPER. ATTACH THEM TO BARBECUE STICKS AND PROJECT THE SHADOWS ONTO A WALL. NOW, YOU CAN PERFORM YOUR OWN STORY OF THE BEAR AND THE ANT.

4

BAMBOO EXPERIMENT: ASK FOR AN ADULT'S ASSISTANCE TO OBTAIN A PIECE OF BAMBOO. EXAMINE IT CLOSELY AND TRY TO FIND OUT HOW MANY LEAVES IT HAS, WHAT ITS TEXTURE IS LIKE, AND IF IT'S HOLLOW ON THE INSIDE. THEN, WRITE OR DRAW YOUR FINDINGS ON A PIECE OF PAPER.

5

MASK MAKING: USE CARDSTOCK PAPER, CARDBOARD, GLUE, AND OTHER CRAFT MATERIALS TO MAKE MASKS OF THE BEAR AND THE ANT. CUT OUT THE SHAPE OF EACH CHARACTER'S FACE AND ADORN THEM AS YOU LIKE. THEN, YOU CAN USE THE MASKS TO ACT OUT THE STORY FROM THE BOOK.

6

BAMBOO PICNIC: PREPARE A HEALTHY SNACK, LIKE FRUITS AND SANDWICHES, AND HAVE A PICNIC IN YOUR GARDEN OR AT THE PARK. TO MAKE IT SPECIAL, USE BAMBOO SKEWERS TO SKEWER THE FRUITS OR ASSEMBLE MINI SANDWICHES. TAKE THE OPPORTUNITY TO TALK ABOUT THE STORY OF THE BEAR AND THE ANT WHILE ENJOYING YOUR MEAL!

ABOUT THE AUTHOR

FERNANDA EMEDIATO is a talented and dedicated writer, editor, producer and businesswoman from São Paulo, Brazil. Her passion for writing started when she was only 9 years old, when she wrote *The lost girl*, her first book, in a children's diary. The story, which addresses the importance of not judging people without knowing them, was published by Geração Editorial in 2013.

In 2020, with the support of a culture sponsoring program (Proac) of São Paulo state, Fernanda launched her second book, *The colorless girl*, by Troinha publishers. In that sensitive and caring work, she addresses important topics such as racism and self-acceptance. In 2022, Fernanda published *The bat with no wings*, also through Proac.

The story tells us about persistence and empathy, allowing kids to discover the importance of having dreams and not giving them up.

In addition to her career as a writer, Fernanda has been an activist for children's rights since 2013. She participates in groups that visit schools in São Paulo and other cities, emphasizing the importance reading has in building children's personality.

Fernanda Emediato's dedication and commitment has been finding admirers and recognition in the Brazilian literary and social scenario. Her books contribute significantly to the development of culture and art in her country, and her work as an activist for children's rights inspires many.

LEARN MORE ABOUT HER WORK AT: **www.fernandaemediato.com.br**

About the Illustrated

VANESSA ALEXANDRE was born and lives in São Paulo. She has been working in the publishing industry for over fourteen years as a children's and young adult author and illustrator for publishers in Brazil, the United States, and Europe. She has also illustrated educational materials and created content for advertising campaigns. Vanessa has participated in exhibitions such as Cow Parade and Football Parade, and was one of the artists selected for the 3rd edition of the Refugiarte exhibition, promoted by UNHCR (the UN refugee agency), and was chosen for the New York edition of the Jaguar Parade.

In addition, she performs literary workshops and illustration activities in schools throughout Brazil, implementing activities for students and teachers at events such as the Jornada da Educação de SP, Feira do Livro de Porto Alegre, Feira do Livro de Araras, and the Bienal do Livro, while promoting inclusive education activities.

LEARN MORE ABOUT HER WORK AT: www.vanessaalexandre.com.br

The Panda Bear and the Ant © 2023
Written by Fernanda Emediato
Illustrated by Vanessa Alexandre

1st Edition – November 2023

Publisher and Editor: **Fernanda Emediato**
Cover and Layout: **Alan Maia**
Illustrations: **Vanessa Alexandre**

INTERNATIONAL CATALOGING-IN-PUBLICATION DATA (CIP) (BRAZILIAN BOOK CHAMBER, SP, BRAZIL)

Emediato, Fernanda
  The Panda Bear and the Ant / Fernanda Emediato ; illustrated by Vanessa Alexandre — São Paulo :
Asas Editora, 2023. 32 p. : il. ; 23cm x 23cm. • ISBN: 978-65-85096-21-8 • Título original: O urso panda e a formiga
  1. Children's literature I. II. Title.

23-164563 CDD-028.5

Indexes for systematic catalog: 1. Children's literature 028.5 • 2. Young adult literature 028.5 • **Tábata Alves da Silva
– Librarian – CRB-8/9253** • All rights reserved for this edition. • Printed in Brazil